DOG on WHEELS
at
Sunny Sea

For Magnus

Published by TROIKA
First published 2018

1

Design: Lisa Kirkham

A CIP catalogue record for this book is available from the British Library

ISBN 9781909991712

Printed in India

troika
Well House, Green Lane, Ardleigh CO7 7PD

www.troikabooks.com

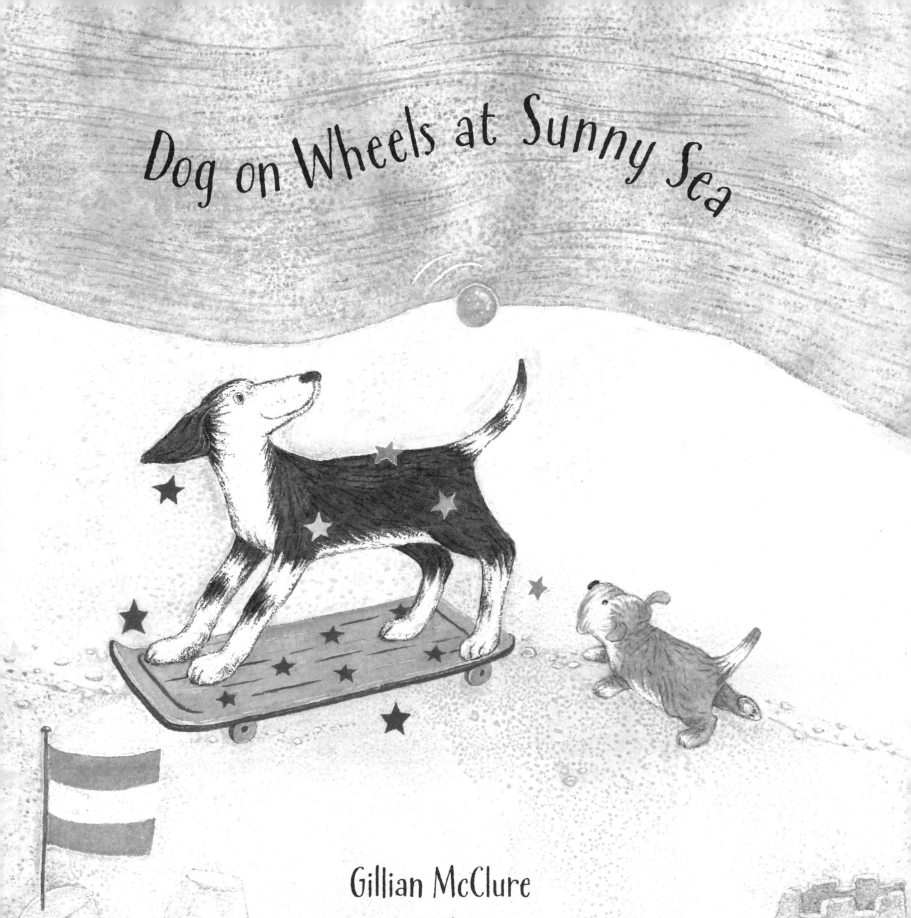

Dog on Wheels at Sunny Sea

Gillian McClure

troika

It's **NOT**

and Todd is making a noise.

'Leave your toys, Todd and come with me,' says Dubbin.

'We'll spend the day at
SUNNY SEA.'

'Let's
roll!

'I'm taking my ball,
my little blue ball,' says Todd.

Two eyes,
two ears
and a nose,

Dubbin has wheels and goes
faster than feet through the heat,

rolling along, singing a song,

looking for somewhere quiet
on the sands at Sunny Sea.

Dydh da KERNOW

'This is where we want to be', says Dubbin.
'A hot sleepy spot right by the sea.'

But Todd can't stay still.

He's b o u n c i n g his ball,
his little blue ball,

UP and DOWN,

UP and DOWN.

SPLAT!

'QUICK!

Pick up your ball, Todd.
Follow me!
This isn't at all
where we want
to be,'
says Dubbin.

Oh NO!

Todd picks up a ball,
not blue but red
and hurries
away.

Two eyes,
two ears
and a nose,

Dubbin has wheels and goes
faster than feet
through the heat,

rolling along, singing a song,

looking for somewhere quiet
on the sands at Sunny Sea.

'This is where we want to be,' says Dubbin.
'Somewhere with lots to do and see.'

But Todd can't stay still.
He's b o u n c i n g his ball, his little red ball,

ROUND and ROUND
and ROUND and ROUND.

CRASH!

Oh NO!

'QUICK!

Pick up your ball, Todd.
Follow me!
This isn't at all
where we want to be,'
says Dubbin.

'We'll find somewhere else by Sunny Sea.'

Two eyes,
two ears
and a nose,

DANGER

Dubbin has wheels and goes
faster than feet through the heat,

rolling along, singing a song,

all the way to the pier at
Sunny Sea.

'This is where we want to be,' says Dubbin,
'enjoying the view at Sunny Sea.'

But Todd can't stay still.

He's b o u n c i n g his ball,
his little red ball,

HIGH and LOW and OVER the wall...

Dubbin races down to the beach.
Todd is just out of reach.

He rolls into the sea
and calls,
'Grab hold of me!'

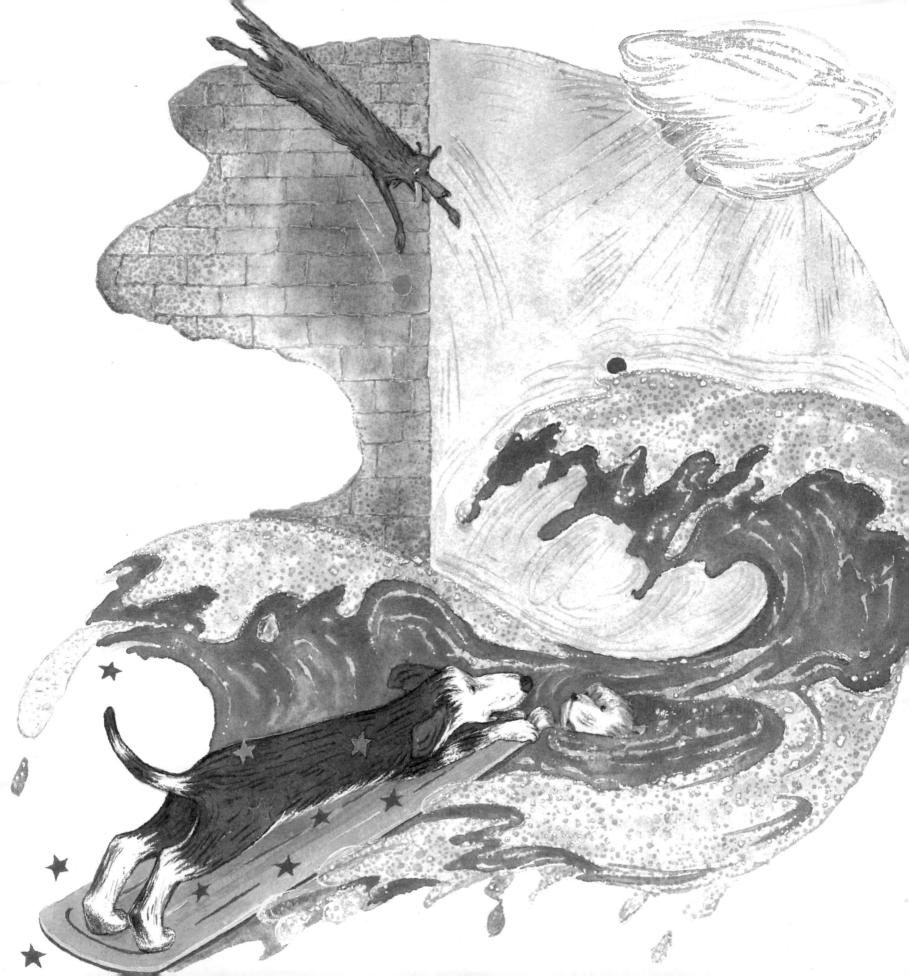

Two eyes, two ears and a nose, Dubbin is up on his board and goes floating fast without a mast,

surfing a wave,

FEARLESS and brave,

on the
SPARKLY
Sunny Sea.

They WOOSH in on a wave

and
LAND
on the sand.

Then Dubbin looks around.
'This is exactly where we want to be.
Away from it all, beside the sea.'

And there, washed up, is a ball,
not red but blue.

'Take it, Todd,
and I'll play with you,'
says Dubbin.

And together they race, over the sands,

bouncing the ball,

the little blue ball,

rolling along, singing a song,

HAPPY to be at SUNNY SEA.